THE CONVENT

THE CONVENT

A Moral Tale

Rosamund Coakley

AESOP Modern
Oxford

AESOP Modern
An imprint of AESOP Publications
Martin Noble Editorial / AESOP
28 Abberbury Road, Oxford OX4 4ES, UK
www.aesopbooks.com

First edition published by AESOP Publications
Copyright (c) 2016 Rosamund Coakley

A catalogue record of this book is
available from the British Library.

First edition 2016

ISBN: 978-1-910301-25-8

Prologue

EVERYONE called me Misty except my mother, my aunt (who knows everything) and the Headmistress. When my father's friends met me for the first time they often said to him, 'What an unusual name. How did you think of it?' and he would smile and say, 'I didn't.'

Before I knew Wilf, he called me Missy, because, so he said, 'I was a right little miss.' My mother did not like this, nor did my aunt who believed we should keep the name given to us at the font for the rest of our lives and no one had the right to come along and change it. This caused a falling out between Wilf and my mother. It upset him no end and when he could bear it no longer he told his mother about it.

She said it could easily be settled by changing my name to Misty after her favourite flower, Love-in-a-Mist, and I was never sorry.

CHAPTER ONE

THE CONVENT was large and dark. It had tall pointed roofs with huge chimney stacks balanced on top. None of this frightened me, but if I was entering the Convent to become a nun, I felt there'd be no escape. It stood close to the road and had a short half-moon drive for cars bringing parents and girls to the school. The porch was small with a latched front door, which made me want to see inside.

A timid little maid answered my mother's ring. The entrance hall had a short flight of wide steps covered with a lovely moss-green carpet. The handrail curved at the top to join each wall, like a balcony rail.

'Come with me,' said the little maid in a 'chapel whisper', as if we were expected.

We followed her up the stairs onto the main corridor and were shown into a room which she called 'the garden parlour'.

Shortly after closing the door I heard a loud ringing of a bell. It rang twice, stopped, then rang once. My mother sat down and I went to gaze out of one of the windows, which looked onto two grass tennis courts and flower beds. Between the windows was a small locked door with steep steps leading down to the garden.

Two pictures hung on opposite walls, both very serious. One was of the Pope and the other the Founder of the Order. I had seen different orders of nuns before and knew their habits consisted of plenty starch above the waist and heavy serge garments below, with beads or a crucifix hanging from the waist. My father admired nursing and teaching nuns because they worked. He had no time for priests who spent money on themselves, so when the collection plate came round during Mass on Sunday he put very little on it and he wasn't ashamed.

I sat down and waited for someone to come. Everything seemed so still as if no one ever went in or out except the little maid to dust. I didn't know what time it was as my mother never wore a wristwatch although she had one.

When the Headmistress entered we stood until she sat down. My nails were clean and I was tidy so I didn't mind her having a good look at me. The reason for this visit was not to enquire about my schooling but about the uniform. My mother didn't like it. She thought it ill-fitting and dowdy because it made thin girls sag and fat girls bulge. I hoped she wouldn't say this to the Headmistress. Her intention was to ask the Headmistress if instead of the uniform I could wear something of her own making. I thought, but dared not say so, that this would not be allowed and I liked the uniform and felt I could look quite smart in it if I tightened the belt.

Before engaging in conversation with my mother the Headmistress asked me if I would like to see their garden. I glanced at my mother before saying, 'Yes please,' and stood by the door leading to the steps.

'Girls do not use these steps,' the Headmistress said. 'They are for visitors,' and pressed a bell.

What a lot of bells in such a short time, I thought.

The little maid appeared again and was instructed to take me to join two other girls who were 'walking round the garden'. One of them had broken her glasses and was not allowed to read or move without somebody with her. I went with the little maid along the corridor and down a stone staircase to a side door, again small. At the door she stopped and pointed to where I should go, saying she wasn't allowed to go any further.

When I joined them, the girl in charge didn't seem at all pleased to see me.

'New girls don't come in the middle of term,' she said in a bossy voice.

I wasn't sure how to answer as I wasn't a new girl yet so I said, 'Oh?' and then pointed to some flowers which looked lovely and asked what they were called.

'They're lupins,' she replied. 'Have you never seen them before?'

'No, I couldn't have or I would have remembered the name. When is that girl going to get her glasses back?'

'When they're mended, silly.'

After that I didn't dare ask her any more questions in case she called me 'silly' again, so I asked the girl who had broken her glasses if she would have to get new ones and she said she didn't know.

This 'walking around the garden' took about ten minutes because we had to go slowly. If this was what school was like I wouldn't mind being here. I had told my uncle several times that I didn't want to go away to a boarding school. He always laughed and said, 'The nuns will make a tame lassie out of you.'

*

We had walked round the garden twice when the door from the parlour to the garden opened and the Headmistress clapped her hands and signalled for me to return. When I did we were taken to see the chapel which was along the other end of the corridor. The steps to the altar were also moss-green and the flowers were like ones I had seen in the garden. All the benches had spaces for missals and prayer books. Only a few old nuns were saying prayers and they were at the back of the chapel. It was so still and silent, the only sound came from the flickering of the sanctuary lamp.

Later, when we had left the Convent I asked my mother if I would be wearing the school uniform. She said not unless I wanted to look dowdy. So I supposed she would make two sets of dresses for me, one for the winter and one for the summer. I told her about the poor girl who had broken her glasses.

'Your father never broke his,' she replied.

*

I became a new girl that September and was given the number 69. I wore a nut-brown dress with a pleated skirt which spread out when I skipped. Being new I was put in the charge of an older girl in the class. It was a small classroom and had double desks and high windows. The class mistress had her desk on a dais and looked very stern. I shared a desk with the girl in charge of me. I didn't like her because she was always bossing me.

During an arithmetic class the nun saw me counting on my fingers and told me I must stop it at once. I didn't, because I couldn't count any other way, I didn't know how, so I counted under the desk. We had reached the seven times table and the nun asked me what seven times seven was, I said I didn't know. She told me to come up to her desk and hold out my hand and she slapped the palm with her ruler. I didn't mind – it didn't smart for long.

Some girls were so quick with their answers I wondered how they did it so I began to remember what the tables looked like and that was how I got through the nine times tables — the worst one of all. But whenever I could I used my fingers.

*

One day the nun said she had a surprise for us. She did this occasionally with a box of chocolates which she passed around the class just before the bell went for tea. We would save the chocolate and spread it on our bread to make it last longer. This time she was going to show us a real silkworm. I wasn't keen on going near anything that wriggled or looked like a caterpillar. She had the silkworm in a closed box on a windowsill. When she raised the lid I could see it was quite fat and the girls gathered round to look at it. Some said it was yellow, others that it was grey. I kept wondering what would happen if it got out of the box and, of course, it did.

The nun was very upset and had us looking everywhere for it. I was afraid I would accidentally touch it and then I would scream. The gardener was called and he said it escaped by the window and would make a nice juicy meal for a hungry bird. This upset the nun even more. He must have been right because we never saw it again. I would have preferred if I knew exactly what happened to it and for several nights I always examined my bed before I got in.

*

On Sundays we always wrote our letters home. I was quick and always had much to say. The bossy girl took ages to get started and would twist a piece of hair around her finger trying to think of something. After a few lines she would stop and try to think of something else to say and this was the Sunday after the silkworm escaped. After that I always thought of her as the Slow Girl and began to like her.

It was the same way in the sewing class which I loved. She sat next to me. I was knitting something for myself and she was embroidering a tray cloth. It had a lovely pattern with bunches of flowers at each corner. She had managed to do a few of these but it took her ages to thread a needle and change the coloured thread. When the nun wasn't watching us I would do some chain stitch or French knots for her. But I loved knitting and could spend all day doing it. My mother sewed beautifully and what I knew I learned from her.

Knitting she did not like. She told me 'it would get me nowhere' and if I wanted to knit I'd have to teach myself, which I did when she bought me a knitting book. Being good at knitting didn't really matter, being good at lessons did. During our French lesson a visiting nun came into the class to see how we were getting on and to show her, the class mistress asked me what *pomme de terre* meant.

I wasn't sure but thought it sounded like pomegranate. The Slow Girl shot her arm up immediately to show that she knew, and she did. I thought, she may know the meaning of *pomme de terre* but I knew what a pomegranate was like. My father bought one to show me. He cut it in two and let me taste it.

The visiting nun said to the Slow Girl, 'Very good' and to me 'You must try a little harder.' I'd like to have known the right word and was disappointed that the Slow Girl did and I didn't.

*

Later that day, just before tea when I thought we might be getting a chocolate, the class mistress asked us to pray for one of the house sisters who had just died from a growth in her throat. I thought what a terrible thing that was and began to feel my neck for anything that might be starting to grow.

The nun told us the poor house sister was not able to swallow – 'Not a bite', she said, 'and now God has released her from all suffering.'

That made it sound even worse and I wanted to look into my throat the minute I could. So before tea, I rushed down to the cloakroom and got as close as I could to the mirror. My throat looked the usual pink with that funny little thing hanging down in the middle. That made me feel better and I rushed up to the refectory in case I should be missed.

During tea I tested my swallowing to see if everything I ate went down without stopping and it did. Then I realised I should be praying for the poor nun, not thinking about myself.

I would ask Wilf about this during the holidays. He would explain it without thinking me silly.

CHAPTER TWO

FTER CHRISTMAS we got a new headmistress. The upper school nicknamed her 'Don't Do It Again'. She was always seen hurrying along the main corridor with papers in her hand and her veil flapping. If she passed you, you would feel a breeze. When girls were told to report to her in her study for breaking some rule she never got cross and just said, 'Now run along, and don't do it again.' So nobody minded being sent to her study; it was better than sitting in class and if no-one saw you, you could dawdle on the way back.

During the previous Christmas term I had made friends with the girl who had broken her glasses. She was in the class above me but would always wait in the corridor at mealtimes so we could go into the refectory together although we sat at different tables. She told me she was knitting a bedjacket. I was interested in the pattern because it was done in one piece by changing to different-sized needles. It would be quick to make and I could knit one for myself.

I was always cold in bed, especially my feet and shoulders, and the nuns wouldn't let me have a hot water bottle. At home I always had one although my father said I'd be better without it. He never felt the cold like I did. He told me when he was studying in Scotland the landlady had no fire in the room where he had his breakfast, so he warmed his hands on his boiled egg and this made him used to the cold. He didn't like people smothering themselves in clothes. If the school uniform didn't have a scarf he wouldn't let me wear one. Of course my mother paid no attention to what he said and so long as I looked good in a scarf she wouldn't mind me wearing one but never wore one herself or got a sore throat because she didn't.

*

None of the girls liked the Easter term because of Lent. The class mistress told us Lent was a preparation for Easter. That's alright for priests and nuns. They have big tummies and can store food in them. But our tummies are small and food in them doesn't last very long so Lent for us meant no jam for tea except on Sundays and an extra fish day on Wednesday, but the pudding was my favourite.

It was a jam tart, half-filled with yellow jam and half with red. I liked the yellow part best but as I sat towards the middle of the table by the time it got to me only the red jam part might be left. We never had yellow jam at home. My mother didn't like jam and my father had wild blackberry jam. He picked the berries himself during August. I had rhubarb jam because my father didn't believe in fancy jam.

*

Before we broke up for the Easter holidays instead of reading about the Passion and Crucifixion and learning bits by heart the class mistress acted out the whole story for us. We could listen and watch her and not do any work ourselves. She put her hand on her hips and stood and spoke like a man. It sounded so real she was able to make us believe we were listening to Pontius Pilate. I wondered how she could do this while still being dressed like a nun.

I had been to pantomimes at Christmastime and loved them but they were never real, they had happy endings. Sometimes if the class was good or finished before the tea bell went she would read or tell us a story and I could think about it when I was in bed. My mother read me stories but would hurry through them to get to the end quickly. She read me *Alice in Wonderland* but I didn't like it. I thought Alice a very silly girl. I'd have done something about it.

*

During the Easter holidays I told my uncle I wanted to learn how to swim. Every Wednesday afternoon during the summer term all the girls who wanted to swim in the Baths were taken there by the nuns and I wanted to go too. He told my mother everyone should know how to swim but she wasn't keen. She didn't want me to develop 'muscular shoulders or heavy legs and become unsightly'.

My uncle said this would not happen. I knew she could swim but didn't do so now and she hadn't muscular shoulders, although she did like a good shoulder not a sloping one. My mother usually listened to my uncle and bought me a smart bathing suit and a pretty bathing cap.

I went to the baths the first Wednesday after I went back to school for the summer term. Two nuns went with the girls to the baths and sat in the front row of tiered seats to watch them. The swimming instructress was small, round and very pink. If my mother had seen her she would never have let me learn swimming. She told us we should try and swim like mermaids and showed us how. She swam from one end of the pool to the other under water without making a ripple and returned on the surface without a splash.

She began by teaching me the strokes and putting her hand under my chin and my front. I was dying to be able to swim but felt if she took her hands away I would sink. After twenty minutes of everybody shouting and splashing, the nuns told us it was time to come out. Before we returned to the convent we were counted and when we got back we were each given a Mars bar. This didn't spoil our tea as we were always hungry.

*

Playing in the garden was the best part of every day. It wasn't like an ordinary park garden where everything is in order and there is nothing left to discover. Of course the grass tennis courts were kept special for matches and sport's day and to be seen and admired from the parlour windows by visitors. But our garden had been left to itself. No one disturbed or tried to change it. So we played wherever we could and found a place for everything. We played rounders on an old asphalt tennis court which had become cracked and bumpy with daisies growing out of the cracks.

In winter we played netball on the hard tennis courts. In summer we practised tennis against the brick walls of the laundry. On flagstones no longer used for netball we skipped at one end and the small girls played hopscotch at the other. Near the old asphalt court was a raised garden with flower beds separated by crazy paving. Pansies and other small flowers were at the front and lupins and tall flowers at the back. In the centre was an arch of roses. This part of the garden was to be looked at, not played in and was out of bounds for us.

At the back of the raised garden was a steep grassy mound and a shady path, walked daily by the nuns when they took their recreation between one and two. Our recreation after dinner was a dull walk. The only excitement that ever happened on these walks was if we met the Chaplain. It threw everyone into a flurry, especially the nun who walked at the back of the rank with a girl on each side of her. It was the only time we saw the Chaplain without his heavy vestments on and he looked quite smart, almost a different person. It was this that caused the flurry.

CHAPTER THREE

ALTERATIONS were made to the hem of my dress for the new Christmas term. I was in Class 2 now and wouldn't be bossed any more. The classroom was smaller than the last one and had single desks with plenty room inside. I liked the class mistress: she didn't have a stern face and spent more time on spelling and writing than sums and tables. The Slow Girl was put in charge of filling the inkwells and giving out blotting paper; another with opening the windows. I wasn't given charge of anything. A tree grew outside one of the windows and reached as far as the bathroom window on the floor above. I loved watching the branches sway on a windy day and listened to the sound they made when they rubbed against each other.

*

Early in the term the Lower School were to be given a prize for whichever class had the best stand in the Christmas sale of work. There were three classes and I was certain ours would easily win. If I didn't have to do lessons or could knit during them I could have three jumpers ready in time. I told the sewing nun we could win if she let me decide what we should make – I would have managed the sewing class far better than her. She took an age to wind a ball of wool and it made her get very hot.

I said I could knit jumpers, some could knit tea cosies and others knit one-piece bedjackets and with the odd bits of wool she kept in a basket we could make tassels or bobbles for the cosies. Those who couldn't knit well could make coloured scarves. The Slow Girl who was very neat – that's what made her so slow – said she would sew up my jumpers, and if I did her French knots she might manage a tray cloth in time.

'Oh please, Sister, let's try,' the class pleaded.

'Oh very well,' said the nun, 'but it will keep me very busy.'

I don't believe she was ever 'very busy' or knew what it meant but she let me have the wool for the first jumper. I picked green with an orange fleck and started right away. I could race through the rib and then follow the shaping pattern the nun gave me. My aim was to get halfway to the armhole before the next sewing class when the nun would give me another ball of wool.

I had to think of some way of carrying the knitting around with me without it being seen. The sewing nun would never notice if I put the work back in my cubbyhole or not. If I wore my cardigan I could put the knitting inside my dress and the cardigan would hide it.

In winter after supper we had our recreation in the hall and made a lot of noise dancing around to records brought back by the older girls. The particular nun in charge wouldn't notice where I was and if she didn't see me would think it was my bath night so I sat in a corner alcove knitting near another girl who was busy writing. I asked her what she was doing and she said copying out 'The Charge of the Light Brigade'. The library nun had allowed her to borrow a book for this but never asked her why she wanted it. It looked a very long poem to me.

Her name was Berry, or that's what she was called and had seen Errol Flynn in the picture and wanted to read all about it. She said she would do another copy for me because I also had seen the picture. She had been to see it twice but my father didn't like me going to the pictures in case I picked up an infection so I couldn't go often. If I could, I'd go every day. He loved the pictures himself and went with my mother on his half-day. He liked Edward G Robinson, Fred Astaire and Ginger Rogers but not Joan Crawford. My mother liked James Cagney, George Raft and Greta Garbo. I'm sure the little maid went to the pictures whenever she could but wouldn't talk about it. The nuns didn't like to hear the girls talking about film stars.

Most nights when the nun wasn't watching I sat in the alcove knitting while Berry copied the poem. She said she read it in bed every night until the lights went out.

*

I was on my second jumper when Don't Do It Again left. We were all very sorry because she never punished us. The older girls said she was too lax with girls who broke the rules and that's why she went. The new Headmistress put a stop to shouting and sliding along the corridors but it was some time before she got the nickname Prickles. She didn't rush around but held herself together, not in a stiff way but in a tight way. She seemed to like looking for trouble so we were always on the watch for her.

In chapel she knelt on a prie-dieu at the very back and could spot any girl who talked and they would be spoken to afterwards. She always wore a 'clicker' in her waistband so she never had to raise her voice. Any girl who needed a 'long sleep' in the mornings was made to go to bed after supper without any recreation. She was told: if you are unable to get up with the rest of the school in the morning then you need to go to bed early. When she supervised us at supper it meant she had something to say about a rule that was broken. Nobody liked her and I wondered about my knitting.

In class I kept the knitting in my desk at the back of the books. The green and orange fleck looked lovely and after doing one jumper I would know the shaping by heart and could work more quickly on the second. I wanted to make a jumper like this for myself during the Christmas holidays and would ask my mother to take me to a shop where I could look at flecked wools.

The sewing nun liked the first jumper I did and told me to do the next in the same wool. The Slow Girl had sewn it up beautifully but was terribly slow with her tray cloth. We got a visit from the headmistress to see our work. I don't think she knew much about sewing or knitting. I had put double French knots in some of the flowers in the tray cloth but she never remarked on them and I thought they made the flowers look lovely.

Spelling was now as difficult for me as tables. In our first lesson we were told to write down the spelling of three words all very alike: bus, busy and business. The last word I had never come across, the first I knew but the second I didn't. My desk was next to a clever girl's and she had written down the answers in no time. 'Busy' sounded like 'bis' and I wondered had it one 's' or two. I chanced two and added a 'y'. I didn't see why a girl in the Lower School should be expected to know how to spell business, so I did very badly.

The next lesson was worse. We had to make up sentences with 'does' and 'dose' in them. I could do the sentences easily but wasn't sure about 'does' and 'dose'. After a few more lessons the nun gave us a spelling test and said to me before we began that if I made any more mistakes between does and dose she would send me down to the pharmacy for a nasty dose of medicine. I felt this nasty dose would be cod liver oil. I didn't take it but some of the girls had to and they hated it. They'd put a little salt at the tip of the spoon to try and take the taste away. So I was careful not to make mistakes in the test.

The next trouble I had was with 'how' and 'who'. I could not separate them, they were so alike. The nun said to me, and I still liked her, that she had lost all patience with me and I was to write out each word fifty times during my recreation after supper. That meant less time knitting.

I sat next to Berry who was still copying out the poem when another girl came to speak to her. She was older than us and turned out to be Berry's sister, Thea. She was in the upper school and said to be very clever. Her uniform looked sloppy and the collar wasn't put on right. If she tightened the belt and fixed the collar she would look better. I told her about 'does' and 'dose' and 'how' and 'who' and how it stopped me doing my knitting.

She said I needed to read more. I said I don't need to when I can think of Errol Flynn. She had a small fat red book in her pocket and said to me that before she left school she would know every word in it. She showed it to me. It was a French dictionary and each page was crammed with words. It really amazed me that she wanted to learn all those words when she didn't have to.

*

We had been studying the Catechism to prepare for a visit from the Chaplain and the class mistress told us we must be word perfect. He would examine the Lower School in Catechism and the Upper School in Scripture. He didn't look that strict although his sermons seemed so long when we wanted to go into the garden and we couldn't fidget because the Headmistress would see us. Before he was due, she came to examine us herself. We preferred the class mistress – she always prompted, but the Headmistress wouldn't. Every word had to be the right one and it was the small words that gave the trouble.

On the day she came I had nearly finished the back of the second jumper. When my turn came to be asked a question I couldn't get it word-perfect and no-one dared prompt me. If the class mistress had asked me the question I could have answered it perfectly. The Headmistress seemed to pull herself tighter and went on to the next girl. As she left the classroom she came to my desk and said, 'Show me your Catechism.' I opened the desk to get it out and she saw the knitting. The needles were sticking out from the back of the books.

'Give that to me,' she said, so I did.

'Where should it be?'

'In the sewing room.'

'That's where you will take it. First you will rip it.'

'All of it?'

'To the last stitch and stand up while you are doing it.'

No-one in the class dared move and I didn't want her to see how upset I was. It was almost the whole of the back. I ripped it to the last rib row, but cast on stitches are difficult to unrip. The Headmistress brought out a scissors attached to a cord in her pocket and cut the wool.

'Now return it to the sewing room.'

But I didn't. The sewing room was through our cloakroom and I thought the sleeve of my coat would be a good hiding place. When I wore my coat I could put the knitting in my shoe cubby-hole, that way I could get at the knitting whenever I wanted. I had to finish the jumper quickly and start on the third to have them ready in time for the Sale of Work so Berry always kept a lookout while I was knitting.

*

Before the sale of work began, the Community came into the hall to look at our stands and give their opinion on which was the best to the sewing nun. Sister Anthony was one of the first. She looked after our clothes and trunks and gave us spare hankies left behind by old girls when we had colds. She always sat at a huge table piled with clothes back from the laundry. In winter she wore mitts and I often saw her rubbing her knees when she was sewing or mending. She was looking at the bedjackets while I was arranging the stand and said to me how warm they'd be if you were sitting up in bed. I said I could easily knit one for her during the Christmas holidays.

'Oh, I would have to ask Mother Superior first, although one of the sisters was allowed to keep a travelling clock she was given. She was being sent to one of our Houses abroad.'

'Couldn't you say I made it specially for you? I would do it in white.'

'Mother Superior wouldn't object to that,' and she felt the bedjacket again. 'I like to read my prayer book in bed.'

Poor old nun. I'd think of a way to make the bedjacket warmer. The trunk room in which she worked was on the same floor as the music rooms. An unusual spiral staircase lead to it from the front of the dormitory. A stone staircase went from the ground corridor up to the music rooms, passing on its way the far end of the dormitory. The music rooms were supposed to be haunted by some saintly nun. No girl would walk through them at night because of the strange noises made by the glass partitions.

*

Our stand in the hall had the most people looking at it because it was so different. If we had made more things they would all have been sold. The Slow Girl had finished her tray cloth in time and we made ragdolls from leftover material found in the sewing nun's cupboard. These sold first and by the time the sale was over all the stands were bare. The visitors were waited on by the Lower School assisted by Tiny who served them tea from our refectory teapots while we passed round trays of angel cakes.

The sewing nun was congratulated several times. This made her very happy and also very hot. I'm sure she would have liked a cup of steaming tea but the nuns never eat in front of us. Sister Superior, who we seldom saw except at school concerts and prizegiving, arrived with the Headmistress and was joined by the sewing nun.

After the arrival of Sister Superior the noise and excitement died down. The sewing nun passed her a piece of paper while we waited for the result. Sister Superior stood up, looked in our direction and smiled. We had won the prize.

*

Next morning Sister Anthony was in the classroom with the class mistress. We were told our prize was to be photographed. I expected the prize would be a big box of chocolates but this was like a surprise half-day and would be forever. I hadn't had my photo taken for a long time and I'd like to see how I looked now. Sister Anthony was here to see our clothes were right. Some girls had to change their cuffs and collars and we all went down to the cloakroom to tidy our hair. I supposed we'd sit in the hall on chairs used for concerts with our hands folded on our lap and try to look like angels. When we were all ready Sister Anthony gave us a final look and was satisfied with our appearance.

After our 'break' the photographer arrived. He looked at us and said to the class mistress, 'These are the flowers of tomorrow' – Berry's sister, Thea, would know what he meant – 'The grounds are out, it's too cold and a school setting is out, flowers need room to bloom.' The class mistress wasn't pleased with his remarks and said to him, 'This leaves you little choice. Please remember we are a school.'

Then the sewing nun arrived looking hot and excited as if she had only just heard about the photograph. She expected it would be taken in the hall and that she would sit in the centre of the group. The photographer also told her a school setting was out of the question.

'So where do you plan to take it?'

'Sitting on the front hall steps.'

'Not in my opinion a suitable choice.'

'It's a perfect setting.'

'Then I shall require a chair.'

'That's completely out. These are flowers not furniture.'

'All these girls were under my tutelage for this prize.'

'Under or over, Sister, it's all the same to me. I'll produce a picture that will stun you.'

I was surprised that anyone dared speak to a nun like that. He told us to follow him along the corridor and bring some exercise books with us. We stopped at the steps leading to the front hall and were told to group ourselves, keeping a few exercise books on our lap and leaving the rest by the railings. While we were getting settled a few nuns had gathered on the main corridor to see what we were doing. The sewing nun had brought the headmistress who looked very tight.

The sewing nun said to the photographer as he was getting his things ready, 'I don't know what Sister Superior would think of this arrangement. No one has ever sat on the front hall steps. They are not meant for sitting.'

He told her he was not a 'yesterday's man', Superior or no Superior. Another nun suggested a potted plant at the bottom or top of the steps. He shook his head and said, 'Potted plants are for dark corners and dull parlours,' then waved his arms about to tell the nuns to move away. We were to look towards him, but not at him and smile as if we saw someone we liked.

It was nearly half past twelve before we were finished.

I'm sure the nuns would talk about this all during their dinner, if they were allowed to talk. During dinner the girl at our table who never talked in chapel and walked around in a pious sort of way said she would like to marry someone like the photographer. It amazed me that she knew what she wanted already; we all thought she'd become a nun.

*

When the photograph came it was mounted and could only be touched by the nuns. We saw ourselves as we never expected, not stiff but real. I never knew you could take a photograph like that. The mounted one was to be framed and kept in the classroom and we were to have four copies each with special envelopes for ourselves.

The Slow Girl didn't know what she'd do with the extra copies. I knew. Wilf would get one, he'd be so delighted to see me growing up. I'd keep one and send the other two to my mother so she could send one copy to my aunt who had a very plain daughter.

Sister Anthony came to the class and said it was the best school photograph she had ever seen. The sewing nun also came and said it should have been taken in the hall with all of us seated properly. She wanted a yesterday's photograph from a 'yesterday's man'.

CHAPTER FOUR

IN EARLY January my mother got a letter from the Headmistress telling her I was to return to school for the Easter term in school uniform. I didn't mind because I thought I would look quite good in it and if I became head girl my uniform would always be perfect.

My mother didn't like the Headmistress, and said her mind and appearance were not in keeping with her position. I was so afraid that when the dresses arrived from the shop which supplied the uniforms she might start altering them and the nuns would notice and say something to me. When they did come she said she had no idea who they were meant to fit and were beyond doing anything with. There was no 'give' in the skirt and it would develop a 'seat' in no time. As she folded them back in the box she said a soldier's uniform, bad as it was, would be better made.

*

I was busy knitting during the holidays. I loved sitting upstairs in front of the fire by myself. This room was used as a nursery when I was small and then when I was older and got measles or had a cough, I would sleep there with the door open so my father could hear if anything happened during the night. It was such a cosy room I could stay there all day.

After I had finished the jumper for myself I began on the bedjacket for Sister Anthony. I asked the girl who broke her glasses where she got the pattern from. She said her mother found it in a magazine and gave it to her. I decided on the large size as nuns probably wore heavy nightdresses and used a thicker wool so she would never feel cold again.

My mother always did her sewing in this room because the light was good and she wouldn't be disturbed. The room had a lovely gate-leg table. I planned to have one like it when I grew up. I wrote my letters here. It never interested my mother who I wrote to, or what I said or how bad my spelling was. I rarely saw her write and when she did she used a relief nib and no-one could read her writing but myself. I wrote with a backhand and the nuns kept telling me I must write upright.

Some girls had very neat handwriting and spent ages putting in full stops and commas. I could never do anything slowly as my mother hated to see anyone dawdling.

In the evenings I looked at film books. My mother always got them for me during the holidays. I loved reading about film stars, what they were doing and who they were marrying. There were always photographs of scenes from their latest pictures which I might have seen. I cut these out for my album and saved some for Berry.

*

After Christmas, my mother took me to see *Mother Goose*. It made her laugh and I saw something I had never seen before. It made me decide what I'd like to learn. A man, dressed like a gypsy, sat at the side of the stage near the footlights and now and again played what seemed like a large accordion. He played without music the most wonderful tunes and smiled and looked at something that wasn't there. If I learnt to play like that I could never be unhappy and if I wore an attractive dress I might be asked to play at concerts and parties.

When I mentioned this to my mother later she said the straps would ruin my shoulders and I should learn the piano. That would make me sit up straight. Most girls did learn it, so I suppose I would too. A few learnt the violin and were really keen about it although it always sounded scratchy to me. When I told my uncle about the accordion, he said it was a noisy instrument and learning the piano would be more useful to me but my heart was set on what I heard at the pantomime and it was not noisy.

*

Most girls arrived back for the Easter term in time for tea; the rest were in time for supper. Afterwards we gathered in the hall for recreation and talked about our holidays. When Thea saw me she said I looked good in the uniform and I could tell from her face that I did. She said she had an idea during the holidays which would improve my spelling and at the same time help her with her French vocabulary – she even had that little book with her: I was to give her a word in English from it and she would have to give the correct word in French.

I asked her why Berry wasn't back. She said Berry had a cough and would be back when she was better. I was very disappointed, I had photographs of Errol Flynn to show her. She had given Thea a letter for me which I put in my pocket so I could read it when I was alone in bed. It was then Thea asked me if I would be her 'best friend'. I had none since the girl who broke her glasses left but as I was still in the Lower School and not clever I said, 'If you like, but Berry and I will always be friends.'

She told me she had read two good books during the holidays. One was *Anthony Adverse* and the other *Hatter's Castle*. I said I didn't like names, especially Christian names beginning with a vowel and asked if *Hatter's Castle* was about top hats and castles. The title made me think of the Mad Hatter and the castles I'd seen in fairy tale books.

'Yes, but in a different sort of way,' Thea said.

She had a peculiar sort of smile that stopped before it became a proper smile. That night I thought of Berry and wished she was back.

*

February 8th was our class mistress's feast day. Their feast day was like our birthday.

We gave her a sweet holy picture and put our names on the back so that whenever she looked at it, she would remember us. When she came into the classroom we wished her a happy feast day. She thanked us and said she would keep the holy picture in her missal. Then she wrote on the blackboard: 'Your favourite holiday.'

I liked essays. They were easy for me, especially if I liked the title.

The Slow Girl put up her hand at once and asked, 'Should I begin with the journey?'

The nun said, 'Begin wherever you like,' so I wrote about a hermit crab.

I loved looking into rock pools in a cove I knew well and when I sat on the rocks watching the waves as they broke and splashed, I felt I was in some magical place. No one came to the cove, there was little sand and not wide enough for anyone to swim. The cove looked its best when the tide went out and left everything glistening.

I spent my time looking into these pools watching shrimps darting about and hiding under the seaweed. I watched a hermit crab moving along the damp sand and wondered where it was going when it stopped close to a shell like its own. It suddenly left its shell and got into the new one. It was hardly in when it was out and got quickly back into its own shell. I had never known hermit crabs did this.

During these few seconds it had no shell to protect it and I thought of what the gardener had said about the poor silkworm. Some distance from the cove was a lighthouse and on foggy days if you couldn't see it, you could hear it. At night before I went to sleep I watched the light flash and then fade. It was a wonderful place and a wonderful holiday.

*

The lower school classrooms were on the main corridor and when we came out of class at dinnertime there would always be a few house sisters waiting at the far end, beyond the chapel, for the teaching nuns to join them. They gathered in a group and looked as if they shouldn't be standing there. One of them stood out from the rest.

She was good looking and wore her habit well. She was known by us as Venus.

We never saw the house sisters in our part of the school except in the dormitory at night and we rarely spoke to them except when asking permission 'to be excused' just before we got into bed and they would nod their head. They were always nice to us except Venus. She was very strict if she caught us talking. This was strictly forbidden in the dormitory.

I could never be tidy with my clothes. I saw no reason why I should spend time folding them on my chair after I took them off when I had to put them on again in the morning. So I put my stockings in the form of a cross on top of the pile hoping when the nun came round to see if we were all in bed she wouldn't notice and she didn't.

One nun slept in each dormitory but we never saw them. They came after we had gone to bed and left before we were called in the morning at quarter past six. A girl saw one once and said she wore some kind of cap. I thought the worst thing about becoming a nun was having your hair cut off. It must make them look awful. But perhaps they didn't have mirrors.

*

I often wondered what the house sisters did all day. The teaching nuns did help with the washing up after our dinner. They rolled up their wide sleeves and put on check aprons. Tiny, the refectory nun was small, like the little parlour maid. Even before we sat down after saying grace she was in with the dinner dishes. Although small, by leaning backwards she could carry in scalding teapots to each table for breakfast and tea. Then she would go round to all the tables with a different teapot pouring out tea for girls who didn't take sugar.

I loved tea and always had two cups. I was not at the same table as Thea but knew she didn't take sugar and took salt on her porridge – that I could never understand. It might be the reason why she never smiled properly. My father took a little brown sugar or treacle on his porridge and would take no more than half a teaspoon of sugar in his tea or coffee. He always made a fuss if his tea was too sweet and say he couldn't drink it. I knew the exact amount he wanted and always shook the spoon until it was just under half-full. It never bothered my mother how sweet her tea was so long as it was very strong.

When Berry didn't come back in a few days I wrote a note to her in the hall during recreation and gave it to Thea to put in her letter when she wrote home on Sunday. I made it up in an envelope shape and kept it flat so the nuns wouldn't notice a bulge in Thea's letter and wonder what it was.

That Sunday I wrote a note to Wilf and put it in my home letter. Cook said he came to the back door every

Tuesday to see if there was a note for him. He worked for my father and never had an idle moment. If I was ever alone in the house in the evening when everyone was out Wilf had to come and sit with me. This wasn't often and I loved it because he showed me card tricks – my mother hated cards – and would let me stay up long after my bedtime.

He taught me to ride my bicycle because my father was too busy and my mother couldn't run because it hurt her feet, but she would look out of the window to see if I had fallen off. Wilf never let me fall or topple over. He told me that he had a serious illness when he was young and could never ride a bicycle so he walked everywhere or went, if he had to, by bus.

When I had scarlet fever he came to visit me in hospital but had to stay outside and look in a window. The nurses moved my bed so I could see him. He held up a comic he had brought for me so I would be sure to get it. While I was finishing the note to Wilf the nun in charge told me to hurry up

When I was writing letters the time went so quickly, I had so much to say.

CHAPTER FIVE

GRASSY cliffs stretched beyond the cove with the rock pools and I often sat there alone in the afternoons to watch the sea and listen to the skylarks overhead – I was thinking about that while getting the Catechism out of my desk for a religious lesson when the class mistress arrived and we all stood up.

'Put your Catechisms away,' she said. 'This morning I want to speak about honour.'

What a change from having to listen to the same old questions or repeat the same old answers. I'd heard about girls in the upper school getting Honourable Mention in their exams but didn't know exactly what it meant. Still it sounded better than not getting a mention at all.

The nun began with 'Honour has no rules.' Well, that really surprised me. I thought everything had rules to stop you doing what you wanted. My mother always said rules were meant to be broken when she didn't want me to wear the school uniform. The class stayed very still waiting for her to go on.

'Imagine you are alone, completely alone in a room with a letter lying open on a table. You can read it, even pick it up or you can ignore its presence as if it were a book or pencil. No-one is watching you. You are free to choose. You may say to yourself: I might as well take a look. What harm is there in that? It can't be important if it was left open and I won't tell anyone what it says. So you glance at the letter, read a line or two and then a few more... Did you listen to your conscience or give in to curiosity? Always listen to your conscience. It is your only guide. In life honour will not be as simple as the example I have given you today.'

So that's what honour is all about.

'Honesty, unlike Honour, has rules and you all know what those are. Remember there is no difference between a small or a big lie. Both are meant to deceive.'

Then she wrote on the board: 'A gold medal won by cheating is like a crown without glory.'

The Slow Girl put up her hand and I wondered what she was going to say. She asked if it would be a lie if she said she saw six elephants in the garden. Everyone laughed but herself. The nun said certainly not. No one would believe you and it is free from deception.

Another girl, who always knew her Catechism and never talked in chapel, asked if the saints ever told lies. The nun said few go through life without telling one. Well, my father would tell one if he thought it was for the best. I wouldn't tell one and Wilf could never tell one.

*

During our 'break' at quarter past ten we stood around a refectory table. One Nice biscuit was placed beside each empty cup. We collected our biscuit and took the cup to the nun who partly filled it with watery cocoa. Some girls dipped their biscuit into the cocoa. I didn't because I liked to taste the biscuit.

While drinking my cocoa the Slow Girl came up and asked if I would do her a favour. I didn't mind and wondered what it could be. She wanted me to help her write a letter to her aunt to thank her for a birthday present as she couldn't manage to write two letters on a Sunday. If I knew what she wanted to say I could do it in a few minutes during recreation in the hall after supper, and give it to her in time to copy on Sunday. So I said, 'What will I write?'

'I have to thank her for a birthday present I didn't like.'

I wasn't surprised she couldn't write the letter and said, 'Just thank her for the present and then go on to something else.'

'No, I couldn't do that. She'll be expecting me to say something about it and will tell my mother if I don't mention it.'

So I said, 'What was it?'

'A small purse, not much use to me.'

'Was there anything in it?'

'No. It was empty.'

'You could keep your rubber and pencil sharpener in it,' I suggested.

'I suppose I could – I'll write that then but it will only fill two lines.'

'Well, mention how useful it will be at school, keeping your rubber and pencil sharpener together – you needn't say any more.'

'All that will take me so long,' she said.

'You could end with, "I hope to see you soon."'

'I won't say that. She's coming to visit us shortly, worse luck.'

'Then leave that out and say something like, "The garden looks lovely with yellow and white flowers."'

She seemed pleased with my suggestions, but if the nun caught her copying from the note, she would recognise my handwriting and we'd both be in trouble.

*

During Sunday letters I looked to see how the Slow Girl was getting on. I had never seen anyone write so slowly. The nun in charge was busy reading something so she wouldn't notice anything. Sunday was a day for reading about the Lives of the Saints so that's probably what she was reading. It must be very dull reading about good works and deeds all the time.

Berry had sent a note to me in Thea's letter asking if I had seen any Errol Flynn pictures during the Christmas holidays. I hoped to but I hadn't, although one was on. My mother said I could go and see it one afternoon with Cook. Because of the snow we had to walk all the way and when we got there we were told that because of the snow the film never arrived, so Cook took me to Woolworths instead.

I had a wonderful time looking at all the things. Cook bought two pink garters for herself and then we walked home in the snow. I knew my father was against garters and told my mother I must never wear them at school.

*

Thea had told me Berry was convalescing. I knew what that word meant, I'd heard my father use it. So I wrote my note to Berry on Saturday night in time for Thea to enclose it in her letter home on Sunday. I knew she'd be disappointed about the Errol Flynn picture so I told her we could enter for the three-legged race on Sport's Day next term and start practising for it as soon as she got back. We were much the same size – I was left-handed except when writing – so we would hold each other with our strongest arm.

When I'd finished my letter home I looked again to see what the Slow Girl was doing. She was putting her letters into envelopes so the nun hadn't noticed anything.

Next morning after breakfast I went into the garden to skip. I had to hurry to get my favourite spot on the flagstones. Thea finally found me and arrived looking very glum. She said she was in no mood for this senseless jumping up and down, so we walked around the garden instead.

She was most annoyed as Venus had confiscated her torch that night. I knew she studied the dictionary under the bedclothes but not until the nun had turned the lights out and left and the sleeping nun arrived, and she wouldn't notice anything because she never came out of her cubicle. Thea must have turned the torch on just before Venus left and it showed up on the ceiling.

'Having no torch will ruin me,' she said.

'The next time she's in the dormitory ask her for it back,' I replied. 'It belongs to you. What good is it to her? Nuns aren't supposed to own anything.'

'She won't give it back because she knows I'll only use it again.'

I never saw her so annoyed so I said, 'Then when Berry comes back ask her to bring one with her. I've seen small ones like fountain pens. My mother has one.'

'That's smart thinking and Venus will never suspect,' and she gave one of her half smiles.

'Perhaps Venus hasn't got a true vocation and that's making her nasty,' I said, 'the way Prickles was over my knitting.'

While Thea was busy looking up the French for vocation I said, 'It could be due to a broken engagement and Venus was so upset she entered a convent.' I'd heard my mother speak of a 'broken engagement' and wondered what it really meant.

'If that's what you think then it's her own lookout. There are plenty more fish in the sea,'

And I thought, there is only one Errol Flynn. The French for vocation turned out to be exactly the same and Thea pronounced it for me. She could add this to her store of words which might never have happened if the torch hadn't been confiscated.

'I'll never know it all before I leave.'

'You're making too much fuss over that dictionary. You'll know enough. That's all that matters.'

'No! It's not *all that matters*. I must know it all. I want to read French books in French', and she counted the number of nights she'd have to 'endure' before Berry came back with the torch.

'I can hear you for longer in the hall and pick out really hard words to test you,' I said.

'Until I get the torch, you'll have to, but it's not the same as looking up words myself when I'm in bed.'

We'd been talking behind the mound. This was quite high so you couldn't be seen from anywhere in the garden. The grass on it was always sprinkled with daisies and in summer the gardener brought out benches. It was a lovely place to sit, although I never saw the nuns sitting there. Perhaps they did when the school closed during our summer holidays.

*

A few days later Thea told me that Berry was going to convalesce in a place with plenty of fresh air. Sister Anthony had told me the bedjacket I made for her kept the chill off her shoulders so I asked Thea if Berry would like one – I could do it very quickly.

'If you want to,' she said. 'She might be cold where she's going.'

Then I wondered how I'd get my notes to Berry. Thea said to give them to her on a Saturday and her mother would enclose all the letters when she wrote to Berry. This satisfied me.

In bed that night I thought I'd write a little bit each day. That would give her more to read and tell her what we were doing. So when I wrote home the next Sunday I asked my mother to send me some thin notepaper, some pink wool for a bed jacket and a small torch, like the one she had, and to wrap the torch in the wool and send it all as soon as she could. I could rely on my mother so explained why I needed the wool urgently.

When the nun wasn't looking I had to ask the Slow Girl how to spell 'urgently'.

*

Later that Sunday I was in trouble with Prickles again. She caught me shouting as I ran down the stairs, two at a time, to Thea who was at the top. We were all rushing down to the cloakroom after tea to get our veils for Benediction. Prickles supervised supper that evening – always a sign of someone's wrongdoing – and spoke to me afterwards. She said my voice could be heard in the Chapel even when I was in the garden and this disturbed the nuns at prayer. She asked me if I shouted at home.

'No, Sister,' I said. 'There is no need,' and there wasn't.

This made her stiffen. It was rude of me and my mother would not have liked to hear me say it.

'If I hear your voice raised again in any part of the Convent,' she said, 'you will observe a twenty-four-hour silence unless spoken to by the Sisters.'

CHAPTER SIX

As MY MOTHER disliked pale colours the wool she sent was rose-pink, but would suit Berry's hair. It was golden brown with stray wisps around the ears. Thea had thick brown hair and mine was dark. I used a hairband. Berry was lucky she didn't need anything. Thea had a side parting and used a strong clip.

Immediately the parcel arrived, I asked the sewing nun if she could get permission for me to knit during evening recreation in the hall. She said she didn't see why I couldn't get the knitting done during the sewing class. I told her Berry was sick and needed the bedjacket now and it was such a lovely colour I didn't want to keep her waiting.

'Oh, I don't know,' and she shook her head. 'Sewing and knitting must be done during the class. That is the school rule.'

'But Berry needs it now, not at the end of term.'

'All this "getting permission" is going to be troublesome for me when I have so much to do. I can but try.'

I'm sure the sewing nun never had 'too much to do' and that if I could speak to Sister Superior myself she would agree to what I asked, but the girls never spoke to her, she was too important. I never once saw her in the main corridor. I was disappointed the sewing nun seemed so half-hearted as if it didn't matter, when it did matter.

I had to wait a whole day before I got the answer. The sewing nun said I was only granted permission because of the 'exceptional circumstances'.

When the girls saw me knitting in the hall and found out why, all Berry's class offered to do a few rows each night to help me. It looked lovely when it was finished and the rose colour made it different from other bedjackets. The nuns sent it off to where Berry was convalescing with a note signed by all her class. Thea said she would have helped if she could, but she couldn't and she wasn't going to try and she was glad I'd finished with all the knitting.

She had an important class exam before we broke up for Easter and although she now had a torch I spent a lot of time each evening in the hall with her and this dictionary. We sat in the alcove so the nun wouldn't see us and if she did miss us she might think it was our bath night. The only nun who knew all our bath nights was Prickles.

I told Thea if she didn't stop bending over books she'd get round-shouldered and look awful in a nice dress. She told me she must excel in this exam.

'Excel' was a new word to me. I suppose it meant good or better. She told me what it meant and where it came from. I thought words were always there and didn't come from anywhere. How could they? They were like the rocks I sat on and the sea. She said Latin was essential for me but I wouldn't learn it till I went into the next class, Sister Veronica's, and after that I'd be in the upper school.

That year would also be Thea's last. She planned to read *Madame Bovary* during the Easter holidays and told me I should read *The Three Musketeers* if I could put Errol Flynn out of my mind.

*

Before the end of the week the Slow Girl asked me in the hall if I could help her with another letter. This time it was to a cousin she didn't like. I said I don't like my cousin either so I don't write to her.

'That's what you should do – don't write.'

'Oh, but I must. My mother likes me to write and a letter is due from me.'

'Well, you could write about school and your needlework and how you are looking forward to the Easter holidays. All that will take up quite a few lines. Then go on to the class photograph that we had taken. You could write a lot about that, at least half a page.'

'But what is there to say? It's only a photograph.'

'Explain where it was taken and that the nuns didn't think it was the right place for us to sit, but we all thought it wonderful when we saw it.'

'Yes, I could write about that I suppose. But could you do a copy? It mustn't be too long or she'll expect a long letter next time. She'll show it to her mother and her mother will tell mine.'

No wonder she found writing the letter so hard.

'The photograph bit is sure to interest her and she might ask you to send a copy in your next letter. That would mean you could write less and just tell her the names of some of the girls in the photograph.'

'You won't mention this to anyone?'

'No, why should I?'

'It all takes me so long.'

'When you do your exams try and write faster. You won't get everything you know down in time.'

'I don't know if I could. It's just not in me.'

I said I'd always help her if she wanted and I'd give her the note by Saturday.

I wrote my note to Berry each day in class if I could, but mainly in the alcove in the hall. I asked her to send me her address so during the Easter holidays I could send her photographs of Errol Flynn from my film books. They were the next best thing to going to the pictures. I told her we still had blackcurrant jam, which I didn't like, for tea on Sunday and thought the nuns grew blackcurrant bushes out of bounds to stop us eating them and then made the jam during our holidays. I asked her about her cough and what medicine she had to take. I had nasty coughs too but they never took so long to go away.

*

When Thea saw me writing to Berry she said she didn't know what I had to write about and began complaining about her Maths nun. She said she was 'mentally lazy' and the only thing she did was to water her plants on the windowsill, write a problem on the blackboard for them to solve then sit down and wait for the bell to ring. They learnt nothing from her and were left to their own devices. I had never heard of mental laziness and always thought you were either lazy or you weren't. Did the two types of laziness come together? Thea said I'd have to work that out for myself.

The night before her exam Thea gave me the French dictionary as she didn't want to have it in her possession and told me to avail myself of it while I had it. I did glance at it now and again to look at words I'd marked in pencil, words which she had trouble with. Somehow French didn't appeal to me but I had to learn it, just like the piano. You had to make funny faces to pronounce certain words and this made you look silly. I'd like to have been taught Russian. It would open a door to another place where I would learn about things which now I could only imagine. Everyone knows something about Paris, I know nothing about Russia.

*

Whenever I happened to see the little maid in the morning she was busy cleaning the hall porch, the two parlours or polishing the school bell. This was kept at the top of the front hall steps and rung for change of class and if any nun was wanted. The school nuns had their own bell sequence. Prickles bells was two rings, a pause, then one more ring.

The main corridor was swept every day as we tramped along it morning and evening to and from the Chapel and Prickles couldn't bear seeing a spot lying on it. Our end of the corridor had a large stained-glass window above a wide windowsill. I had only seen this kind of window in churches, they were always of some religious scene or other and tended to make the church gloomy.

But this window was quite the opposite of gloomy which surprised me for a convent. In one corner was a large cluster of deep purple irises with touches of yellow ones appearing here and there. The stems were hidden by leaves which glistened as leaves do after a shower. I often saw the Art nun gazing at it and she rarely left the art room or came near our end of the corridor except on the days she helped to wash up the dinner plates. She said to me once I should study the colour, especially when the sun struck the glass and I did whenever I passed if only for a second.

*

The downstairs corridor ran under the main corridor and although the same it felt completely different. It was dark because it had no windows and the further you went the darker it became.

The junior cloakroom was just round the corner from the stone staircase. The best mirror, low and wide was here, also a large furnace which made noises like gushing wind but no one seemed to mind. Our hair was washed here once a month. The brushes and combs were soaked and rinsed in buckets. All this took up a whole afternoon.

Further along the corridor was the Pharmacy. We liked going there as the nun was never cross and we could talk as much as we liked. If some girls had to take medicine after supper and the nun wasn't there she would leave it out with the girl's name beside it. Of course she was always there in the mornings when certain girls had to take cod liver oil. I don't know how they swallowed it.

Girls with colds were given a coarse lump of sugar with a drop of eucalyptus on it and girls with coughs were given a special medicine. The Pharmacy was as far along the corridor as we were allowed to go, but it didn't stop us looking.

We knew the Kitchens were further along because of the clatter and seeing strange nuns with their sleeves rolled up going in and out. The Kitchens were on the garden side so some light came through to the corridor when the doors were opened. Sometimes I glimpsed the little maid there, looking for something to eat I suppose.

There must have been a short stairs, which we never saw, going from that part of the corridor up to the front hall so the little maid could answer the telephone or front door bell quickly. The 'phone was at the top of these stairs enclosed in a cubbyhole. No one would notice it unless they heard it ring or knew of its whereabouts, so the little maid could rest there without being seen.

Beyond the kitchen the corridor became much darker and led to the nuns' quarters. The Pharmacy nun always came and went this way. And that was all there was to see. The opposite wall was bare until it ended in the senior cloakroom, the one I used. The door, always open, faced the bottom of the stairs so there was always a rush from the stairs to the cloakroom. It had a large fireplace with a heavy fireguard. The fire was only lit on hair-wash days for us to dry our hair.

Along the side of the cloakroom, including the sewing room, was a long corridor leading to the upper school classrooms. Both this and the corridor above it, leading to the recreation hall, had wider than usual windows with radiator pipes below them. On cold days when the nuns weren't watching we would sit on them.

Few nuns came down to the cloakrooms. The only regular nun was the 'Walking Nun'. She would appear in her cloak and gloves and stand by the garden door waiting for us to line up in pairs so we could leave the Convent by the side gate and enter the road in an orderly manner.

Of course Thea didn't like all this aimless walking so she began to complain of a headache and told the Walking Nun she had one. The nun told her to remain in the recreation hall and sit quietly by an open window. She repeated this story once again and was allowed to do the same as before. Now the nuns knew she was studious and thought she might be straining her eyes trying to see the blackboard. She was told that if the headaches continued permission would be sought from her parents to take her to the oculist in town. Of course this never happened.

*

The two staircases used by us were of stone and I cut my knee when I missed a step while running down one and had to go to the Pharmacy. The Pharmacy nun's bell was rung so I knew it must be serious. I pressed my hankie against the knee to try and stop the bleeding.

When the Pharmacy nun came she said I'd have to see the school doctor. I dreaded this. She brought out a roll of cotton wool. This gave me a fright, I thought I might bleed to death. I wished Wilf was with me now, I'd feel much safer. The nun held my knee steady and I closed my eyes and tried not to breathe while the school doctor put the stitches in.

Afterwards he told me I was very brave because I never winced and that my father could take the stitches out during the Easter holidays.

That Sunday I wrote a note to Wilf to tell him what happened to me as I knew he'd like to know and he could see the cut for himself when my father took out the stitches. My mother would not like me to make a fuss about nothing. She had no time for mollycoddling.

When Thea saw me with a bandage on my knee she said it was all my own fault and the only good that came out of it was that I learned to spell 'wince' and she learnt the French for it.

CHAPTER SEVEN

THE EASTER holidays were short yet my aunt wrote to my mother asking me to knit a cardigan for her daughter, my cousin. She also sent the wool. I thought it very lazy of her not to knit the cardigan herself. I'm sure she had nothing else to do.

I found a pattern for a plain cardigan with pockets in my knitting book. I began on the back right away. To make it slightly different I decided to do the pocket fronts in Blackberry stitch to make them stand out. That would delay me but it would make the cardigan admired and my cousin couldn't say she made it herself. I was never going to knit for her again.

Cook had a sister who came twice a week to spend the afternoon with her. She sat on an old flour bin and knitted all the time. It was she who showed me how to do pockets and rib the last few rows to keep them tight. I told her what I was going to do with the pockets and she said, 'Oh, I wouldn't do that if I were you, dear, it's best to follow the pattern', but of course I didn't. She said she'd sew up the cardigan and put the buttons on. That would save me a lot of time and she was as neat as the Slow Girl.

I liked talking to Cook as she always talked about the pictures. Her favourite film star was Clark Gable. She said no one could touch him. Her sister Cissy – a terrible name – who didn't go to the pictures as often as Cook, liked Spencer Tracey. A lot of the girls at school liked these two stars.

When I asked Wilf about his favourites he said as a boy he loved Will Hay so much that he couldn't eat with excitement if he knew he was going to see him. His pictures made all the boys laugh so much they would stamp their feet and make such a noise that the manager would come down the aisle and tell them to be quiet. Now he went to all the Gary Cooper pictures but would never miss an old Will Hay one.

*

Two things happened the next day. My father took the stitches out. Wilf came with him and removed the bandage. It did stick but Wilf took it off slowly so it wouldn't hurt. He had everything ready and watched my father. I thought taking out stitches would hurt, but it didn't although the thought of a stitch being pulled out wasn't nice. My father said the cut had healed and only wanted a dab of iodine and a cover.

Wilf did all this. He was slow and careful but he couldn't stay and talk to me as he had to go with my father, and my mother became impatient with him. She wanted him to hurry up instead of taking his time.

Early that same afternoon the dressmaker came. Hot or cold she always wore a coat and it always seemed the same one, navy. She came with the skirt and bodice for my new summer dress done separately because my mother never liked belts. She would sew a band of the same material on the double and attach the bodice and skirt to it using feather stitch. This made it awkward for the dressmaker to fit me, but she was used to my mother's ways.

Even though the dress wasn't finished it looked lovely. I chose the material myself. It was cream with windmills and little Dutch girls in red, orange and green printed all over it. As the dressmaker was fitting me I wondered why her hands were cold no matter how hot the day yet the sewing nun's were hot no matter how cold the day. I couldn't understand it.

*

The holidays were nearly over and I never heard from Berry. I was surprised and disappointed as I had photos of Errol Flynn ready to send her. I tried on my summer uniform dress for my mother to see the hem and it didn't need altering. The dress looked good on me. It was a tan brown and not the dull brown of our winter uniforms. The short sleeves kept the white cuffs clean longer.

Thea never wrote during the holidays. She said she might if I knew French. She had said everything that was to be said before we broke-up and would say all she had to say when we returned to school So I heard nothing about Berry, and Thea had no letter for me from Berry when I returned to school.

*

In class the girl who sat at the end desk nearest to the door was the one who answered it if there was a knock. It nearly always meant that 'something had happened' and the conversation took place in whispers while we remained silent.

When one of the old nuns became ill we were always told about it and asked to pray for her, so a knock was always expected to say the poor nun had died. Usually the girl took the message to the nun and then she would go to the door. The nun would then tell us what happened, a prayer would be said for the repose of the nun's soul and the lesson continued.

This time, when the knock came, no old nun was ill. The girl called the nun to the door immediately and then returned to her desk. When the nun returned to her desk she shut whatever book she had opened, blessed herself and said, 'I have to tell you that God has taken Berry. She died peacefully this morning.'

She died without me seeing her and I broke into a lot of little sobs. They should have told me. All the time I believed she was getting better when she was only getting worse. If I'd known, my father would have taken me to see her. This upset me more than anything else.

The nun called the Slow Girl up to her desk and told her to walk with me six times round the garden and when I came in I was to collect my veil and sit in the chapel until the tea bell went. I couldn't speak to the Slow Girl as we walked round the garden. She offered me her hankie and said she hadn't used it and had a spare one in her drawer. It was still folded in a neat square.

She stayed with me till I went to the Chapel. I sat at the end of one of the benches. After a while all the old nuns praying at the back of the Chapel came up, one by one and touched my shoulder. It was so nice of them. Some may have lost a brother or sister when young and knew what it felt like.

*

Thea was not in the refectory for tea, so she must have gone home. That night I sobbed again. I was in bed when the class mistress came into my cubicle. I was surprised to see her as she never came into the dormitory. She sat at the end of the bed and folded my clothes neatly on the chair.

'Now doesn't that look better?'

'… Yes, Sister, it does,' and she put the stockings back the way I had them, in the form of a cross.

'Dear child, you must stop crying.'

'But I never saw Berry and I have no photo.'

'Thea will find one for you. Now put your hankie away and close your eyes.'

It was sweet of her to come and see how I was. Before me, she must have taught Berry and would feel sad too.

*

The next morning when I went into the Chapel I felt better. The sacristy nun had arranged garden flowers on the altar in a lovely way. All the colours I liked, nothing dark – and a small wreath was placed on Berry's empty place. During Mass I thought of the poem Berry copied out specially for me and tried to think of the exact time and day I first really met her. I must have been either knitting or writing out 'how' and 'who' fifty times. We sat together in the hall all the nights she wrote it. It will always be mine.

*

I didn't enter for any races that Sport's Day. Two girls asked me to partner them in the three-legged race, but I couldn't replace Berry like that. Instead I helped the nuns arrange the obstacles for the obstacle race. Stringing up buns, floating apples in tubs of water and arranging netting to crawl under. Thea tried a running race without success. She said it wasn't worth the risk of twisting her ankle. I did that once and it was very painful. I couldn't run for several days.

Before the end of term I said goodbye to the class mistress. I would be moving to a new class after the summer holidays. Once we moved we never met or spoke to our old class mistress again. We would see them about of course, but that was all. She told me to write to her and I said I would. She had been very nice to me when Berry died. I always wrote to Sister Anthony in case no one else did. I think she looked forward to my letters and would read them during her mending.

CHAPTER EIGHT

THAT SUMMER I decided to knit a cardigan for myself during the month by the sea. I sat low down on the cliffs so I wouldn't be seen and if I remained till teatime I would see the lobster man rowing back, his small boat piled high with pots. He must set them close to the cliffs because I never saw him anywhere else.

People would wait for him to come alongside the pier and watch him unload. Someone might buy a lobster before he went off to sell his catch: I suppose he'll always be poor because his boat is small but then he can row past the caves and the cliffs and hear the splash of the sea. I'd like to have gone with him to see exactly what he did but his boat was so full of pots there'd have been no room for me.

*

Of course if my aunt, who knows everything, saw me sitting on the cliffs she wouldn't like it. She believed in brisk walks. I saw no point in them unless you were going somewhere in a hurry. Because of my mother's sore feet she couldn't go with her on these brisk walks so I had to. She believed in one brisk walk a day and if a strong wind was blowing, the more she liked it. She said it was a great pity that my mother didn't make an effort instead of sitting for hours with her needle and thread. She often talked of a bracing wind. Our bodies, she said, are made for exertion, and 'she should know'.

I thought the person she should be telling all this to was the sewing nun. I'm sure if the sewing nun went out in a 'bracing wind' it would blow her veil off and turn her into a spinning top. If Thea had an aunt like this she would bring out her dictionary and not listen. I was lucky I didn't have to see her often.

When I returned home from my summer holiday I had a lot to do but I waited a day before I began my letters. I showed Cissy my cardigan and she said I was a great little knitter. Then the dressmaker had to come because my uniform had got too short and my mother wanted her to make a new dressing gown for me from some warm material she had bought.

After seeing me in the uniform the dressmaker told my mother I'd be lucky to see it through the Christmas term. My mother wasn't keen on 'seeing it through' any term and decided instead to get two new dresses from the school suppliers, bad though they were. When the dressmaker felt the dressing gown material she said it was a beautiful cloth, but 'she had her doubts'. Doubts about what my mother asked and the dressmaker said she'd never been asked to do a dressing gown before.

'They buy their own or go without. I know you're particular but I have my doubts,' and she made a funny face with her mouth.

I didn't laugh, but I could have. My mother told her to put her doubts aside and measure me, allowing plenty room under the armholes.

From once she started measuring she was herself again and said it would be ready in time for me to take back to school. It felt so warm I intended to spread it out on my bed at night and if the nun said anything I'd do it after lights out. I often thought I'd be warmer in boy's pyjamas. Some girls did wear them and never seemed to feel cold, but my mother mightn't like it.

If I was allowed to have a hot water bottle from the beginning I wouldn't have to be thinking of all this. When I first came to the Convent I was so cold in bed I curled my feet up inside my nightdress.

One night when the House Sister came round to see if we were in bed she asked me where my feet were.

'Inside my nightdress,' I said.

She told me to get them to the bottom of the bed at once and to make sure, she came into the cubicle and gave them a good squeeze which hurt. My father had an old dressing gown. It was a faded moss green with plaid cuffs and collar. He loved it so much that when my mother wanted to get him a decent one he told her nothing would part him from his dressing gown. He told me he had to put it over his shoulders when he was studying in the evenings in Scotland it was so cold, and he laughed when he thought of it. Well the thought of being cold wouldn't make me laugh.

*

Being in a new class and in my last year in the Lower School meant I was growing up. The classroom was the biggest I'd been in. The desks were more apart with plenty room to pass between them and there were three windows. My desk was near the wall, which I liked and I could still gaze out the windows on the far side. I wondered where Berry's desk had been, but didn't like to ask.

The class mistress's name was Sister Veronica but we called her Violet because she always had a small pot of blue or purple flowers on the window sill. She didn't behave in a pious way like some of the nuns who would, for instance, out of habit or respect, lower their voices when they were anywhere near the Chapel. I noticed she had high cheek bones and dark eyebrows. She seemed and acted more like a teacher than a nun.

It was always Violet who walked round the garden with Venus during their recreation. We only noticed that because they never walked round with anyone else. The other nuns didn't seem to walk round with anyone in particular. The little refectory nun was the smallest of all the nuns and carrying big teapots and heavy dishes made her look smaller because she had to lean backwards. I felt one day she would go backwards altogether.

Her nickname was Tiny and it suited her. She had a small reddish patch over each cheek and if we happened to ask her anything she would just shake or nod her head. When a girl knocked a cup of tea over she was out in seconds to mop it up and pour out fresh tea.

She was only in charge of the dormitories once because we played a joke on her. We were supposed to be in bed by a certain time before the sleeping nun arrived. The night she was in charge a girl told Tiny she couldn't get undressed and washed because there was a mouse in her cubicle so Tiny went with the girl to see for herself. Whilst she was looking for the mouse we chatted and dawdled. Of course no mouse was found.

By the time the sleeping nun arrived Tiny was still checking the cubicles to see that all of us were in bed. After lights out we could hear the two nuns whispering for a long time. None of this bothered Thea: the delay gave her extra time to spend on the dictionary.

*

We liked Violet and felt freer in the larger classroom. I was put in charge of dusting the windowsills. The duster was blue and white check, the same as the aprons the nuns wore when washing up. After I had finished, the duster had to be folded perfectly with every corner meeting If that duster had been mine I would have rolled it up and put it in some corner. The Slow Girl was put in charge of collecting the exercise books after a test. The pious girl was given charge of the chalks and blackboard.

Violet could get cross if we weren't paying attention and slap the desk with her hand: She told me I spent most of my time daydreaming and was so good at it that I was to write a short essay on the subject during the evening recreation.

I didn't mind. I often thought of a picture I saw in a storybook. It showed a path going through a wood. In the story a shaggy dog trotted along this path each dawn and dusk, never before or after and never looked to the right or left. The mystery was: Where did it come from and where was it going to? No one ever saw it start, it just appeared and if it was followed, it would vanish.

My daydream had been: where could it be going? And that was my 'short essay'.

*

At twenty past four Violet said we could put our books away as she had something to say to us. She left her desk and stood in front of the class. I couldn't guess what she was going to say. None of us had done anything wrong.

'Whatever takes place in this classroom,' she said, 'remains within the classroom. It is never to be talked about or discussed when you join the rest of the school. Is that understood?'

We all said, 'Yes, Sister,' and that was as good as a promise.

CHAPTER NINE

THE GIRL GUIDES met every Friday. They did look different in their uniforms, but that's all you could say about them. If I became head girl it would look better if I was 'in the Guides'. That would be my only reason for wanting to join them. The Leader, an 'old girl', always joined them for dinner at the head table. She was smart but had no style.

Although I didn't like the colour of their uniform I thought it would look quite well on me because I was a good shape, but it had no life in it. I would have preferred a mustard shade. While eating my dinner on Fridays – it was always fish or hard-boiled eggs in white sauce – I would look in their direction and picture how they'd look if they were in mustard. I'm sure if the nuns were in dove-grey they'd look more attractive and graceful.

I told the nun in charge I'd like to join the girl guides – I was quite old enough – she seemed pleased, looked me up and down and said I'd have to ask my mother first. I knew I'd have to wait for the right moment but I needed to do it early in the Christmas holidays to give her time to take me to the shop that sold guide uniforms. So a few days into the Christmas holidays I told her I'd like to join the guides.

She put down her sewing immediately and said, 'Well, Rosamund, if you want to grow into a hefty woman with size 40 hips, then join them. They spend their time bending down lighting fires and frying sausages and you know your father doesn't want you eating them, and what's more rucksacks are for boy scouts and strong men.' Then she continued with her sewing.

Of course I knew what all that meant but I wasn't too disappointed. I never did ask Berry what she thought of the girl guides and Thea had no intention of joining them. It meant changing in and out of guides' uniform for no worthwhile reason and she wasn't going to do it.

*

Shortly after Christmas my father became unwell and this caused a terrible fuss. I had never known him to be ill before except when he had a cold and then there was a fuss. When he was told he'd have to rest in bed for six weeks and follow a bland diet he became cross and my mother said I'd have to come home for weekends to help her with him and I wondered if Prickles would let me.

Nuns believed if girls were allowed home during term time they would bring back sweets and worst of all 'bad books' which they would pass round if they succeeded in hiding them. Because six weeks was such a long time to have to spend in bed, my father was advised to make good use of his time by reading the Bible from cover to cover, but he had other ideas. I didn't think reading the Bible was a good idea at all so when I went back to school for the Easter term I asked Thea what she thought of the Bible. She said, 'Dabble if you must, but ponder no.'

Soon after the start of the Easter term we noticed the nuns were taking their recreation in a different way. They were walking round the garden in threes, not twos. We always got a good view of them as they came out from behind the mound. Vera and Venus always walked together and seemed to have plenty to say. Prickles would always lead accompanied by one or other of the nuns – never Venus or Violet – it could be the Art nun one day, the Sewing nun another day and sometimes the music nun. But she had a habit of humming to herself and this might annoy Prickles. Of course there would be other nuns but we didn't recognise them.

Then there was Bunny. She did resemble a rabbit, but in a nice way, like a stuffed toy. We knew very little about her. She taught the violin and cello – both instruments had their drawbacks – in a cosy little room tucked away at the top of the spiral staircase just before the trunk room.

By chance I saw the inside of this little room, not many did. I was on my way to Sister Anthony for spare hankies – she never refused girls with colds – and as I passed, a girl was leaving after her lesson and had left the door open. Only Bunny's pupils could use this room and this made them feel a bit above those learning the piano. At a concert her pupils always played in a group, so we knew what we were in for. It was very dull and the cello being the size it was gave off a booming noise. When it ended we all clapped, especially the nuns, but I was glad it was over 'till the next time.

So this sudden change of the nuns walking in threes instead of twos surprised us. As well as that there was no sign of Venus in the garden or the dormitory. She could be sick but that wouldn't change the walking habit of the nuns. I couldn't make it out, but one of the older girls said it was all Prickles' doing. She was jealous of Venus and Violet, the best-looking nuns in the Convent, and the only way she could get satisfaction was to separate them.

Some wondered how she could do this when she was only in charge of us. A very senior girl, not a member of the guides, said, 'The right words in the Superior's ear and a mention of it being "for the good of the School" is all that's needed for Prickles to get her way, so no-one will be waiting for Violet at the end of the corridor when the dinner bell goes.'

I asked Thea what she thought of all this and she said she had more worthwhile matters to occupy her mind.

Some time later — and this was unusual as we were never told anything about the House Sisters or even knew their names — we were just told that Sister Assumpta had gone to join their convent on the south coast and we all knew where that was. A girl's aunt was a nun there so she knew all about the school. I suppose the nuns thought this would stop us talking about it, but it didn't.

*

When Prickles gave permission for me to go home for weekends she said to me the weekend was not to be treated as a holiday, and, as I would miss Friday night study and Saturday morning class, my class mistress would give me homework which must be completed and done properly. I could do most of the homework quickly except the arithmetic.

When I went home for the first weekend my mother said there was no use showing her my homework as she'd be no help whatever. What surprised me was my father was delighted when I showed it to him. He was particularly interested in the arithmetic or, as he called it, mathematics. He said he had been very good at that subject at school and couldn't understand why I found it so difficult.

It was difficult because I couldn't do it in my head. I once saw Wilf – he always had a pencil on him – tot up figures in a flash and think nothing of it, but I couldn't do that. To make things easier for myself if I had to multiply 19 by 4 I'd do it this way:

$$19 \times 4 = \begin{array}{r} 19 \times 2 = 38 \\ 19 \times 2 = \underline{38} \\ 76 \end{array}$$

When my father discovered the trouble I had with arithmetic and I began to wonder how I'd manage later, in the class with the mentally lazy nun, he said I should read a book that had impressed him when he was young and memories of it still did. He sent me downstairs for this book which was always covered in brown paper and kept in a bookcase in the room where he had his breakfast and sat in the evening. The bookcase was small and neat with a glass front. I always liked it just as I liked the gate-leg table.

As soon as I returned he said, 'Open it.'

I was careful in case it fell apart on my lap, but it didn't, it was perfect. The book was red with gold lettering and in the centre was a dark picture of a large dog standing on a rock. It had one paw raised and its mouth was open.

It was this picture that caught my eye at once. Inside were several drawings, all exciting and mysterious. My father said they were called illustrations not drawings and three were missing when he was given the book and another was loose.

'It's a pity they were lost,' I said.

'Yes' he said, 'it was extremely careless with no thought of their value.'

The book was called *The Hound of the Baskervilles*. I wondered what my aunt would think of me now reading one of my father's books. Whenever she spoke of my cousin she said she was a keen reader and young though she was, she was reading *The Mill on the Floss*. Well, if I wanted to know about a mill I'd rather see it for myself.

Wilf always had some murder mystery book in his pocket. It was flat and thin and wouldn't be noticed. He said he could read one a week, and loved them.

*

I got my homework on Friday afternoons. All the girls were somewhere else and I stayed behind as I wasn't going with them. I sat at a desk in the front in case Violet wanted to show me something. This was my second weekend going home and after getting the homework Violet asked me if I'd like to write a short letter to Sister Assumpta and post it on the way home. I thought it a nice idea and said, 'Yes. I'm sure she'd like to hear from someone at the school. She must miss it very much. It was her home.'

Violet said, 'We must accept wherever we are sent, far or near.'

Although I didn't like Venus I felt sorry for her. The rules would probably be the same at the Convent where she was sent, yet everything would be strange and different and she would be without a friend. The first few nights would be the worst. They were for me. I missed my home so much.

'Is there anything special you'd like me to say?'

'Tell her about yourself and how you are getting on.'

'I could tell her we've got new pinafores, much better than the old ones and they look very smart.'

'Yes do. She would have noticed that herself' – of all the nuns Venus wore her habit the best.

'And I could say another house sister has replaced her in the dormitory. She has quite a wide waist.'

'That would be Sister John.'

'I'll mention that so she'll know who it is. I'll tell her I've permission to go home for weekends while my father is sick. Will I say anything else?'

'Yes, that you hope to write again soon.'

'I've told her quite a lot of things. It's short, but it's still a letter.'

When I'd finished I put the envelope inside an exercise book with the rest of my homework. No one would ever know.

*

That weekend I was in charge of my father while my mother was away for the day. The first thing he asked me to do when she had left was to tell Cook he wanted a full meat dinner and none of her milk-puddings. I knew this was not what he was supposed to have. I went downstairs right away to give Cook plenty time to do all this.

When I told her she said, 'I don't hold with that. He wants one thing, his doctor orders another and your mother barely out of the house. This means an errand to the butchers.'

'I could go if you told me what to get.'

'No you couldn't. Your mother wouldn't allow you inside a butcher's shop and you know nothing about meat.'

'I know what a kidney looks like.'

'What good is that? Your father won't touch offal.'

'What's that?'

'Never you mind. There's nothing for it, I'll have to go myself. It'll be cutlets, nothing stronger, so he can get beef out of his head.'

This change upset her whole morning and made her cross. I was afraid to ask her about the pudding. She made lovely jam puffs. My goodness, how her pastry rose. She told me once, she always let the pastry 'rest' so she mightn't have time to make them.

As she put on her hat and coat and prepared to go out she said, 'I hope he won't regret this and end up back where he started. The best thing you can do is stay upstairs and keep him company.'

I had two letters to write before I began my homework. It was my cousin's birthday and my mother left out a birthday card for me to send. I just put my name under the 'Happy Birthday' bit, and nothing else. I felt like the Slow Girl pretending to like someone when you didn't. Thea said, only like who you want. I don't know how the nuns manage, they're supposed to like everyone in the Community.

In the middle of the second letter my father called me, wanting to know if I had given his message to Cook. I said I had and got on with the letter my mother asked me to write for her. After that I started on my homework.

When I had completed half of it I went in to sit with my father. He was very particular about washing his hands before eating, and during his breakfast if the phone rang my mother would have to answer it and if he had to speak he would hold the receiver with his napkin. He would not touch anything before or while eating. But I was used to all this.

So, when Cook arrived with his tray he was all ready. The cutlets looked juicy and she made potato and parsley rissoles to go with them. The pudding was a coffee mould sprinkled with nutmeg. There was not too much of anything.

I was telling my father how far I'd got in the book when I thought I heard voices downstairs. He wasn't expecting anyone, then I heard Cook coughing when I knew she hadn't a cough.

'I think the doctor has come,' I said. 'I can hear him talking to Cook.'

'What! At this hour on a Saturday? It's no time to be calling on anyone.'

'It is him. He's coming up the stairs.'

My father covered the tray with his napkin and said, 'Quick, get the tray under the bed and pass me the newspaper. Open the door and show him in, but don't speak.'

When I returned to the gate-leg table I could hear them laughing. I thought that's a funny kind of visit but it was a sign that my father was getting better and my weekends would soon come to an end.

*

At 4.30 pm all the fuss was over and the house was quiet. My father was having a pot of China tea, I was having a cup of tea and a digestive biscuit and Cook and Cissy were having a pot of tea and some Eccles cakes Cissy had brought.

I loved Eccles cakes, but was rarely allowed to have them. My mother didn't like the look of them and my father didn't want me eating too many sweet things. No mention of the cutlets was to be made to my mother. If she knew what happened I'd never be left in charge of my father again and Cook would get into terrible trouble.

I was late that weekend completing my homework

CHAPTER TEN

A T THE END of May we started to count the days until Corpus Christie. It was a school holiday with sponge cake for tea but best of all was the procession.

The night before, we prayed for a fine day with a blue sky. From early morning the front of the Convent was filled with the scent of garden flowers picked in readiness for the afternoon. Visiting priests came for the occasion and the little maid was busy running between the parlours and the front door.

Violet helped the Sacristy nun with the altar flowers. Venus used to help, she had a way with flowers. I'd often watch her if she was doing them when we were in the chapel reciting the rosary during May and wondered would she be allowed to help with the flowers in the new Convent.

The Sacristy nun served at Mass. She knelt on a small prie-dieu just outside the altar rails. I always waited for her to ring the bell at the wrong time but she never did. If she was absent Violet took her place. We rarely saw the sacristy nun, she never supervised the dormitories. I'd like to have seen inside the sacristy and examined the vestments to see how they were made.

The procession started at two o'clock and began in the Chapel. The chaplain lead, carrying the Monstrance followed by the visiting priests, the nuns and then us. The procession left the Convent and entered the garden by the side door we all used. Waiting there were chosen girls – the pious girl was one of them – carrying baskets of petals which they scattered on the path as the procession moved slowly towards the old asphalt tennis court where an altar had been arranged for Benediction.

It was all so different from the quiet and stillness of the Chapel where Prickles could spy on us from her prie-dieu. As we gathered at a respectful distance from the altar, a light breeze ruffled the priests' surplices. Nothing remained still. After the Chaplain raised the Monstrance for the blessing he recited the Divine Praises but our repetition of his words got lost in the breeze.

At the end of Benediction the nuns became their real selves for just a few moments and seemed pleased and happy. Not Prickles of course, but the priests would have some nice words to say to her later and maybe she would smile, pleased that all her work had been noticed.

*

When the procession returned to the chapel the Chaplain left the Monstrance on the altar so the poor old nuns who weren't able to join the procession could say their prayers in its presence. They had waited all the morning hours for this special moment and could now spend the rest of the day in prayer.

While the priests sat down to a scrumptious tea in the parlour waited on by Tiny and the Little Maid, our minds were on the size of the sponge cakes at the ends of each table and the amount of jam in them. We could easily eat two slices each and not feel full. Tiny's two helpers looked after us. They had to carry round the heavy teapots and didn't know how to lean backwards like Tiny. Girls who didn't take sugar in their tea waved their hands about and called, 'Over here, over here.'

Prickles' duties kept her in the front of the Convent, supervising Tiny and the Little Maid to see the priests' didn't want for anything so we could call to girls at other tables as much and as loud as we wanted. This was strictly forbidden, although we could make signs when the nun wasn't watching. It was all great fun and that was how we spent Corpus Christie.

*

When my father got better he decided that after staying in bed for six weeks he'd recover his strength by walking.

This meant someone would have to walk with him. Because of my mother's feet she couldn't go with him. Wilf couldn't go because he had to be with the assistant working for my father. My aunt would come but she might annoy him by telling him what was best when he already knew. So, my mother asked Prickles if I could continue coming home for the weekend until my father had completely recovered. Prickles said that under the circumstances she would grant permission.

My father was a bit like my aunt in certain ways. I'd been with him on these walks before, although I'd much rather have stayed at home or gone to the pictures. But my father said I should be out in the fresh air, not sitting in a stuffy cinema. Well, I felt I got plenty fresh air at school.

On these walks I'd often say, 'How much further do we have to go?' and he'd say, 'As far as the next bend.' When my aunt heard of his walking intentions she said the best thing he could do, and she should know, would be to take up golf. A friend of hers took up golf after an illness and never had a day's sickness since. Well, I didn't think taking up golf a good idea at all. If he didn't get the ball into that tiny hole he would only come back cross and upset everyone.

When I told Thea that I would be away for a few more weekends this term she was not pleased. Who would test her with the dictionary? She was used to me and had no intention of making do with someone else. I felt she knew enough already. In the exam she wouldn't be expected to know unusual words, but there was no use telling her that.

For a few days she walked around with a glum face. I had to smile – to myself of course – when it was all over a dictionary. So I wrote down some of the awkward words she had trouble with and told her to go over them during the weekend. She became nearly herself again and said she hoped the weekends, like the knitting, would soon come to an end.

*

It was unusual for Prickles to supervise us during dinner. This day she did and it meant she had something important to say. When we had finished, said grace and were about to leave the refectory, she announced she wanted to see 69 in her study at 2 pm. When she wanted to speak to girls in the corridor after supper she always called us by our school numbers – why I don't know. None of the other nuns did.

When Thea heard my number called she looked across at me with raised eyebrows. I returned the look with a shrug. She was rarely summoned to the 'Inner Sanctum', as she liked to call it, and always knew the reason why.

She amused herself by counting the number of books on top of the bookcase near Prickles' desk. These books had been confiscated from 'certain girls' – Thea was one of them – and there they remained until the end of term when they would be returned. These books were considered unsuitable reading for any Convent girl.

Thea would lower her eyes as she listened to a lecture on 'purity of the mind' which, according to Prickles, these unwholesome books attempted to destroy. Thea said that lowering her eyes and looking downcast gave her a penitent look not in keeping of course with her intentions and she left the study giving the impression of being 'truly contrite'.

Prickles often spoke of 'purity' when she took us for religious instructions. She told us, as growing girls we should be aware of the perils awaiting us in the years ahead, especially that of temptation and her voice would then become 'hushed'.

I wondered what these perils were. The only ones I knew of were perils at sea. She said we should pray to the Blessed Virgin and follow her example. Did this mean that nuns were pure because they never married and what would she think of the pious girl who would like to marry someone like the photographer? But Prickles never explained what these perils were and no girl dared put up their hand to ask. I wondered if the confiscated books were all about these perils and that's why they were there.

*

As I stood outside Prickles' door that afternoon waiting for the school bell to ring I still couldn't think why she wanted to see me. I knew she didn't like me going home for weekends in case I brought things back for girls in my class. As I opened the door after knocking I could tell the Little Maid had been because she left a trail of O'Cedar behind.

Prickles was at her desk looking very tight and as I came nearer I noticed she had one of the letters I had written to Venus in front of her and beside it was the envelope. I got a terrible fright and could feel my heart beating but I didn't want her to notice anything.

'You may be seated,' she said, and pointed to a chair.

I thanked her and said, 'I prefer to stand.' I was as tall as Prickles now and felt better standing.

'As you wish.' She held the letter up in her hand. 'This has recently been brought to my attention. Do you recognise it?'

'Yes, Sister, I do – I wrote it.'

'Since Sister Assumpta left the Convent you seem to have developed a habit of writing to her. She was not one of your teachers. You only knew her to see. I doubt if you ever spoke to her.'

'No I didn't, but I thought she might be lonely like I was when I first came here.'

'You were a child then and Sister Assumpta is no novice.'

'During the holidays I might even write to Sister Anthony to tell her what I was doing.'

'And you would be right to do so in appreciation of the care she takes over your clothes. But I am speaking now of Sister Assumpta not Sister Anthony. When girls are placed in our care they are here to learn and obey. One hour is set aside each week for them to write home to their parents and, time permitting, a close relative. You know what day that is?'

'Yes Sister, Sunday.'

'But you are not here on a Sunday and must have written this letter during class time.'

'I never write in class time, only when I have a spare moment.'

'Of these you seem to have plenty.'

'Only when class finishes early and I can be very quick.'

'You could write the letter, if you still felt so inclined, at home during the weekend.'

'Oh but that wouldn't be the same. Sister Assumpta would like a school letter best.' I couldn't say: Because it was written in the room where Violet spent most of her day.

'What Sister Assumpta "likes" forms no part of your schooling. Did you receive any help with this letter?'

'No, Sister, I never need help with letters, only spelling.' and I wondered how Prickles managed to get the letter.

When nuns got anything special they put it in a patch pocket under their white starched 'bib' until they could look at it undisturbed. Then again Venus may never have got the letter – nuns didn't drop or lose things. If a 'holier than thou' nun was in charge of the post she might have noticed that Venus got two letters, close together both in the same handwriting so when another came she felt it her duty to keep it and send it to Prickles.

'I was not aware you knew the names of the House Sisters.'

'But I don't. None of us do.'

'That is strange. You mentioned the name of a Sister John in this letter,' and she picked it up. 'You wrote, "Sister John has taken your place now at night."' She put the letter down. 'How can you explain this after what you have just said?'

'I must have heard someone call her that and when I saw her in the dormitory I just happened to remember it.'

'When did you hear this?'

'I can't be sure. If we hadn't been told that Sister Assumpta had left, we'd never have known her name.'

She picked up the envelope. 'I see this letter was posted here on a Friday.'

'Yes, Sister, we always stop on the way back so my mother can call to the Bakery Shop.'

'Well, Rosamund, your weekends will cease forthwith. Your mother has been notified. In future your letter writing will be confined to Sunday and no other day.'

'Yes, Sister,' and I thought if Prickles ever discovered the truth Violet would get into terrible trouble. Sister Superior would be told and the Mother House informed. I didn't know what might happen to her. Prickles would never rest until Violet was punished. She may be sent to another Convent and none of us would know where she had gone. All I could do would be to write to Venus from home and 'happen' to mention that Violet had left. Sister Anthony might tell me where she'd gone.

Prickles looked at the letter again and then at me. 'You realise an omission is as grave as a lie?'

'I always own up when I have to.'

'So I have been told. The lie I refer to is your reply to my question: Did you receive any help with this letter? The omission is your refusal or unwillingness to explain how you came to know Sister John's name. You said you heard it from someone. I am waiting to know who this is.'

'I might have heard it in the garden or during the Old Girls' "Reunion".'

'Both unlikely explanations. You have behaved in a deceitful manner. You write a letter from this school and unknown to us post it to another convent.'

'I haven't deceived anybody.'

'You have done more than that, you have brought dishonour to the school by your duplicity and will have until tomorrow to reflect. If your answers remain unchanged you will repeat them in the presence of another sister. What has taken place in this study is not to be repeated. You may leave.'

*

When I met Thea before tea everything seemed like it always did, as if what took place in Prickles' study never happened. She asked what all the 'mystery' was about. I said Prickles didn't like me going home for weekends and had stopped it.

'I'm not surprised. She wants order and routine and you failed to conform. Anyway I'm glad. Those weekends left me bereft.'

That was because Thea had a new French book. Not one of her exam books but one she had for her own enjoyment. It had a long title and she said it was about a brief fantasy of enchantment. She kept the translation in a small notebook with the French book in her desk inside another cover. Whenever we were together I never had the French dictionary out of my hands.

One evening when we'd spent a long time over a difficult piece of translation she said to me, 'When I leave I'll give you this little gem,' and she kissed the dictionary.

I had to smile and said, 'But what good is it to me?'

'Because dear one,' she replied, 'we will not come this way again.'

She always liked her little riddle.

CHAPTER ELEVEN

THAT EVENING during study in the hall I wondered which nun Prickles would have with her when I answered the questions tomorrow. The nun would probably not be told the exact reason for her presence. Prickles might not want anything known until she could be certain that Violet helped me with the letter and of this she would never be sure. If the nun was the Art nun, after hearing the questions she would guess what it was all about but keep it to herself. Prickles just tried to frighten me into changing my mind by saying another nun would be present to hear my answers.

I could never let Violet down. If I told the truth and betrayed her, it would stay with me for ever like a stain you can never remove. Prickles would never get the answer she wanted from me or know what happened in the classroom that Friday afternoon. I can still see Violet standing with her back to the window watching me as I wrote the letter.

Poor Violet, I wonder what she was thinking. Then I thought of tomorrow and Prickles. She would try to catch me out over Sister John's name because we never did see or meet the House Sisters except when they supervised us in the dormitory at night. We may notice them when they returned to their places after receiving Holy Communion, but that was all.

At night they would be waiting for us to arrive and always stood in the same place which gave them a good view of all the cubicles. When sounds of splashing and washing stopped and girls who asked to 'be excused' returned, the nun would then move and check the cubicles to see all the girls were in bed, then she said a night prayer, turned off the lights and waited for the sleeping nun to arrive before disappearing.

*

We hated going to bed, especially in the summer and hated being woken by a nun ringing a bell at 6.15 am. She said a morning prayer and then checked each cubicle to see all the girls were out of bed. It was so hard to get up and do what had to be done but worst of all was stripping the bed to 'let it air' before trooping down to Mass.

I heard the nun supervising us call my name.

'Yes Sister?'

'You have not turned a page for the past twenty minutes.'

'Oh – I must have closed my eyes,' and quickly picked up the next book I had to study. We had to memorise a poem, but I could do this quickly because I liked it. Then a fussy girl raised her hand and I wondered what for because no-one asked questions during evening study as the nun who supervised us was not a class mistress.

The fussy girl said she was sitting in a draught and it would give her a stiff neck and she began rubbing it and making a face. The nun had to leave the rostrum and close the window. This took her attention from me. While the nun's back was turned a note was passed on to me from the Slow Girl. Her aunt was sick and her mother told her to write to the aunt but she didn't know what to say.

The nun was quickly back on the rostrum so I couldn't reply to the note but I thought of a way she could write the letter and still keep it short. I knew a nun who kept a box of holy pictures for girls who wanted something special.

I noticed one was different. It was pastel coloured with a little verse at the bottom. If the letter was short the sweet holy picture would make up for it. I'd work out what to say when I got into bed. I didn't have to think about tomorrow, as I knew what I was going to say.

I could feel the nun's eye on me again when she announced we had ten minutes left to complete our study; I was glad it was nearly time as I felt so hungry and supper always filled me up, although we never had tea, only water to drink.

*

It was my bath night that evening so I could get straight into bed. I wanted to get the note to the aunt written before lights out. The Slow Girl could say something like:

I was sorry to hear you were sick. I hope you like the holy picture and will soon be better. I shall pray for you each night until my mother writes to say you are well again. I hope this will be soon.

And so do I.

*

Next day I stood outside the study door again waiting for the school bell to ring. My cuffs were clean and I was tidy. When I entered, Bunny was sitting on a chair beside Prickles. If it had been Tiny I couldn't have been more surprised.

She was in a comfortable position as if preparing to watch, and of course listen, to a school concert. Prickles sat upright and was very tight. She didn't offer me a chair this time. I suppose they could see me better if I remained standing.

I don't think Bunny knew the reason for her being here so she wouldn't understand the reason behind the questions. She was only interested in those string instruments and her own little room. She had no idea what our class was like or what we did any more than Violet would know, or want to know what Bunny did.

That might be why Prickles chose her. She wasn't curious or nosey. I never saw her come into the music rooms and speak to our music teacher who had far more girls to teach and prepare for their exams than Bunny. Whenever I passed her little room I never heard nice tunes, only sounds like scratching and booming. When I glanced at her now, her face gave nothing away and all she could know about me was that I was wearing school uniform.

Prickles said to me, 'You know why you are here?'

'Yes, Sister,' then she turned to Bunny.

'I shall ask Rosamund two questions and discuss matters relating to them. You, Sister, will listen to her replies and take note of them. I expect to hear the truth, not evasion or omission.'

Bunny nodded, changed her position and leaned forward as if to show Prickles she wouldn't miss anything.

So Prickles began. 'Did you receive any suggestions or assistance with this letter?' and she held it up.

'No, Sister. It was my own doing.' I only wrote the letter because I felt for Violet, not for Venus, and I would do the same again.

'You wrote it on a Friday afternoon during class?'

'No, Sister. Not during class but between change of lessons. I had a few minutes while exercise books were collected and fresh books were handed out.'

'It seems strange that when you appear to have so little time you should decide, for some reason, to write to Sister Assumpta,' and she pulled out the letter again. 'It shows no sign of having been written in haste,' and she looked at me.

'I try not to give that impression.'

'And you succeeded.'

'Of course if I was writing to Sister Anthony I would take more time and put more into it.'

'We are not here to discuss your correspondence with Sister Anthony. So your letter was completed before you received your homework?'

'Oh yes. I try not to keep my mother waiting.'

'And when did you get the homework?'

'At the end of class.' Prickles looked at the wall timetable.

'When all the girls had left – and how long did that take?'

'Not long. I could guess what the homework would be and wrote it down earlier. Then Sister would add a poem for me to learn by heart.'

'You seem to have been so absorbed in your letter writing and homework that you could not apply yourself to class work. Your mind was drawn in two directions.

One claimed your attention, the other did not. In addition you broke a school rule. You are fully aware that letters are written on Sunday and no other day. Until this incident no girl has taken it upon herself to start letter writing during class.'

Bunny nodded.

'Your conduct will not go unpunished.' I suppose if she couldn't punish Violet over the letter she could punish me instead. I didn't mind. One day I'd leave school and be free like the skylarks, Violet never would.

Then Prickles turned to Bunny. 'This second question remained unanswered yesterday. Today I expect an answer.'

Bunny nodded then Prickles turned to me.

'You mentioned Sister John's name in your letter. It is strange you thought of mentioning it at all. How did you know the Sister's name? Their names are only known to the Community. So you must have heard it somewhere or from someone.'

'It could have been by chance. Once my father couldn't remember the name of a friend's dog but when he saw the dog again later the name came back to him. So it could have happened to me the day I sent a ball out of bounds. When I went to get it I might have heard someone call Sister John's name and thought no more about it. Then, when I saw her in the dormitory after Sister

Assumpta left I remembered the time and place I first heard it.'

'What a remarkable explanation. What time of day did all this take place?'

'After breakfast.'

Prickles turned to Bunny. 'Where are the House Sisters at that hour?'

'In the Convent attending to their "charges".'

Prickles turned to me. 'You have failed to disclose where you heard the name by withholding the truth.'

'I cannot tell you what I don't know.'

'That is a statement you will not forget, you "don't know" because you choose not to know.'

She turned to Bunny, 'Have you made note of her replies?'

Bunny nodded and gathered herself together.

'Then you may leave, Sister.'

I opened the door for Bunny but there was no glance of sympathy or kind pat on the shoulder. And off she went to her own little room in a satisfied sort of way. How little she really knew. That was the real Bunny, not the one in the toy shop window.

I closed the door and stood in front of Prickles and I lowered my eyes as Theo did as I wondered what punishment Prickles had in store for me.

'I have only one thing to say to you, Rosamund. As long as I remain Headmistress of this school you will never have the honour of becoming head girl.'

I tried not to let her see how I felt. I knew that the prizes and medals would never be mine that would have made up for everything.

Now I would leave school with nothing to add to my name. She – Prickles must have known what I wanted all along.

www.ingramcontent.com/pod-product-compliance
Lightning Source LLC
Chambersburg PA
CBHW071327130626
46556CB00004B/1781